The COTTONWOOD SINGS

Library of Congress Cataloging-in-Publication Data available upon request.
Text and Illustrations © 2023 by Alfreda Beartrack-Algeo

Printed in China

7th Generation
Book Publishing Company
PO Box 99, Summertown, TN 38483
888-260-8458
bookpubco.com
nativevoicesbooks.com

ISBN: 978-0-9669317-1-6
eBook ISBN: 978-0-9669317-6-1

28 27 26 25 24 23   1 2 3 4 5 6 7 8 9

We chose to print this title on paper certified by The Forest Stewardship Council® (FSC®), a global, not-for-profit organization dedicated to the promotion of responsible forest management worldwide.

The COTTONWOOD SINGS

Written and illustrated by
Alfreda Beartrack~Algeo

7th Generation
Summertown, Tennessee

In the beginning
was First Woman.

Her name was Hunku.
Hunku was immortal
and never aged.

All the animals and plants loved to hear her
sing to them. But Hunku was very lonely.

Hunku would go to the riverbank every day and cry herself to sleep.

A certain beaver lived in the river that Hunku visited daily.
Beaver was in love with Hunku.

He marveled at the way the sunlight reflected off her long black hair.

And he was awed how her eyes shone
like chokecherries on an August day.

Beaver pleaded with the Great Spirit
whose name was Wakan Tanka.

"Wakan Tanka," Beaver begged,
"please turn me into a human
so I can be near Hunku."

Wakan Tanka said, "Beaver,
I will grant you your wish
to become a human.

You will be First Man
and will be called Takahe.
But one day you must
return to the river and
go back to being
a beaver again."

Beaver agreed.

Upon awakening,
Hunku was surprised
to find Takahe sleeping
by her side.

Takahe said, "Do not be alarmed, most beautiful one. I have come to you from Wakan Tanka."

Hunku was pleased. She was no longer lonely with Takahe by her side.

They enjoyed their life together.

Hunku gave birth to four beautiful daughters.

The daughters,
being mortal,
grew up quickly
and married the
four sons of Tate,
the Spirit of the Wind.

Each couple
journeyed to one
of the four directions
to form a sacred
medicine wheel.

The eldest daughter married
Eya, the eldest son of Tate.

They moved to the west

The second eldest daughter married Yata, the second eldest son of Tate.

They moved
to the north.

The third eldest daughter married Yanpa, the third eldest son of Tate.

They moved to the east.

The youngest daughter married Okaga, the youngest son of Tate.

They moved to the south.

Unlike their children, Hunku
and Takahe were immortal.

And so they outlived many
generations of their offspring.

Then, the day that Takahe was dreading finally arrived.

Wakan Tanka said, "Takahe, it is time
for you to return to the water
from whence you came."

Hunku cried as Takahe
turned back into a beaver.

Beaver waddled to the edge of the river and disappeared beneath the surface of the water.

Hunku was once again very lonely.

She would go to the riverbank
every day and cry herself to sleep.

Hunku pleaded, "Wakan Tanka,
please turn me into a tree so
I can be near Beaver forever."

When Hunku awakened, she had changed into a cottonwood tree.

Her arms were strong limbs
that lifted high toward the heavens.
Her feet were strong roots that bore deep into the earth.

Tate blew
his gentle
breezes
through
Cottonwood's
dancing leaves.

Cottonwood would sing to all the animals, including a love song to a certain beaver that lived in the nearby river.

To this day, you will find cottonwood trees living near bodies of water and beavers living near cottonwood trees.

ABOUT THE AUTHOR
AND ILLUSTRATOR

Alfreda Beartrack-Algeo is an enrolled member of the Lower Brule Lakota Nation, Kul Wicasa Oyate, Lower Brule, South Dakota. Alfreda is a writer, artist, and educator. She and her spouse reside in Palisade, Colorado, where she manages her studio and gallery, Mato Nunpa LLC.